This is the story of Cinderella. She works very hard for her cruel stepmother and her wicked stepsisters, yet she is always happy and gentle. One day Cinderella meets her fairy godmother and good things start to happen.

Now turn the page and read how Cinderella's life changes forever!

Once upon a time, in a tiny kingdom, there was a gentle and lovely girl named Cinderella. She lived with her cruel stepmother and two ugly stepsisters. They were jealous of Cinderella's goodness and beauty, and made her work night and day. The mice and the birds were Cinderella's only friends.

Cinderella did all the cooking, scrubbing, washing and mending, while her selfish stepsisters did nothing. But Cinderella never complained. She believed that someday her dreams of happiness would come true.

One day, an invitation arrived from the King. That night, a royal ball was to be held in honour of the Prince. Every young maiden in the kingdom was commanded to attend.

Cinderella was very excited.

"That means I can go, too!"

Her stepsisters just laughed.

"But the announcement said every maiden was to attend."

"Very well, Cinderella, you can go – after you finish all your chores. Now, wash this slip for me. Mend these buttonholes. Where's my sash? Press this dress. Curl my hair. Oh, and find my fan."

They kept Cinderella busy all day long. Then it was time to leave.

"Why, Cinderella, it's time to go. You're not even dressed for the ball!"

"I didn't have time to dress."

But the wicked stepsisters just laughed and left for the ball.

Cinderella tried not to feel badly.

"Oh, well. What's a royal ball? I suppose it would be frightfully dull and, and… completely wonderful."

She burst into tears and ran away, into the garden.

"I thought someday my dreams would come true," sobbed Cinderella. "Now I'll never get to the royal ball."

"Yes, you will, child, but we must hurry."

Cinderella looked up, and there stood her fairy godmother.

"Let's see, now," said the fairy godmother. "I'll need a pumpkin and some mice."

Then she waved her magic wand and sang these magic words, "Bibbidi-bobbidi-boo!" To Cinderella's amazement, the pumpkin became a splendid coach, and the mice turned into elegant horses.

"Oh, this is wonderful," cried Cinderella.
But then she looked down at her rags.
"I'll need a…"

"A coachman, of course," interrupted the fairy godmother. And she changed a horse into the coachman.

"Now hop in, my dear! You mustn't be late."

"But don't you think my dress..."

"Lovely, my dear," began the fairy godmother. Then she looked again. "Oh, good heavens, child! You can't go in that. Bibbidi-bobbidi, bibbidi-bobbidi, boo!"

And there stood Cinderella in the loveliest gown she had ever seen. On her tiny feet were delicate glass slippers.

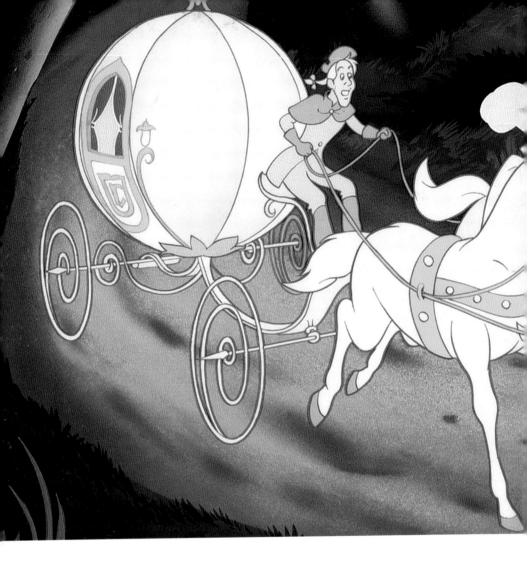

Cinderella was delighted. "Oh, fairy godmother
– it's like a dream come true!"

"Yes, child. But like all dreams, it can't last
forever. On the stroke of midnight, the spell will
be broken, and everything will be as it was before."

"I'll remember," promised Cinderella.

"Oh, it's more than I ever hoped for! Thank you, fairy godmother."

"Bless you, my child. Now hurry up. It's getting late."

Cinderella stepped into the pumpkin coach and was whisked away to the royal ball.

The King's ballroom was magnificent. Every lady in the land was dressed in her finest gown. But Cinderella was the loveliest of them all.

When the Prince saw the charming Cinderella, he fell in love instantly. The Duke said to the King. "You see, Your Majesty, the Prince has danced with that girl all evening. It looks like he's found the girl he wants to marry."

All at once, the tower clock began to strike midnight.

Cinderella cried, "Oh, I almost forgot!" And without another word, away she ran, out of the ballroom and down the palace stairs. On the way, she lost one of the glass slippers, but she couldn't stop to get it. Cinderella stepped into the magic coach, and quickly drove away. As the clock struck for the twelfth time, the magic ended! Cinderella was left with a pumpkin, some mice, and the memory of her wonderful evening.

The next morning, the whole kingdom was wondering who the mysterious girl was.

The only clue was the lost slipper. The Grand Duke carried the glass shoe from house to house looking for its owner, for the Prince had said he would marry no one but the girl who could wear the tiny slipper.

Every girl in the land tried hard to put the slipper on. The ugly stepsisters tried hardest of all! But it was no use. Not a single girl could fit her foot into the glass shoe.

And where was Cinderella? Locked in her room. The mean old stepmother was taking no chances that poor Cinderella would try on the slipper. But Cinderella's mice friends found the key and rushed it up to the locked room. The Duke was just about to leave.

"Well, madam, if you have no other daughters, I'll bid you good day."

Just then, he heard a voice calling to him.

"Please wait! May I try the slipper?" It was Cinderella.

"Of course," said the Duke. "Every girl must have a chance. Please sit down."

He slid the glass shoe onto Cinderella's foot, and it fit perfectly.

Cinderella's dream had come true. No longer would she slave for her cruel stepmother and her foolish stepsisters. She would marry the Prince and live happily ever after. And what became of the little mice who had been Cinderella's only friends? They went to the palace, too. And they all lived happily ever after.